R. Washbourne

The Village Lily

R. Washbourne

The Village Lily

ISBN/EAN: 9783742857613

Manufactured in Europe, USA, Canada, Australia, Japa

Cover: Foto ©Andreas Hilbeck / pixelio.de

Manufactured and distributed by brebook publishing software
(www.brebook.com)

R. Washbourne

The Village Lily

THE VILLAGE LILY.

THE VILLAGE LILY.

𝔗ranslated from the 𝔉rench.

"None ever implored the Mother of God in vain."

LONDON:

R. WASHBOURNE, 18 PATERNOSTER ROW.

1874.

THE VILLAGE LILY.

CHAPTER I.

SEVERAL years have passed over our heads since the events which I am about to describe took place. But it is with certain recollections as with certain affections, they survive all. As for me, Time has changed nothing, destroyed nothing, carried nothing away with him. I live in the past with the dear ones whom I have known and loved. I still hear their voices, they still speak to me, I listen to them. If fresh affections occupy a large place in my heart, they have not destroyed the remembrance of them.

Memory is the religion of the heart, as the love and worship of God is the religion of the soul. If our story have not that powerful charm which the imagination of the relator can add to the recital, it has at least, though simply told, the merit of being *true*. Among the persons whom we are about to introduce to the reader, not one is imaginary; all have lived, and some live still, in the little village where I knew them. This village, called Cercelle, is situated in the most fertile part of the department of the Haute-Marne, and is rich in mineral productions. There almost every commune possesses a brick oven, a factory, or a foundry. There happiness is generally seated at the fire-side of the hard-working labourer, for where work is hard, prosperity reigns.

One evening in the month of March, 1848, the wife and daughter of the blacksmith of Cercelle were awaiting his return. The night was far advanced, the lights of the village had long been extinguished, and the peaceful inhabitants were sleeping soundly. Why had not Mr. Ambrose Durier returned to his home? It was Saturday, pay-day, and for some time Ambrose had indulged in the habit of breaking into his fortnight's wages at the village inn, with some companions he had had the misfortune to listen to. Do not think that these two or three friends of Durier's were the sons of the country; not so. No one knew where they came from. They had arrived at the factory, had asked to be employed, and the superintendent of the works had engaged them. Wherever a great number of hands are employed, there are always men without families whose past history is more or less doubtful. They often come from cities from whose gates they have been expelled. It was with such friends as these that Ambrose Durier, the strongest and best workman at Cercelle, passed his evenings, forgetting his wife and daughter—his wife, whom formerly he had fondly loved, and to whom the villagers had given the surname of *the Good;* and his daughter, the image of her mother, and whose gentle influence ought to have sufficed to keep him from his evil ways. But Ambrose had bad acquaintances. He had learned to *drink,* and when intoxicated he forgot that there are duties which every man is compelled to perform unless he wishes to become criminal.

The room in which Jane was waiting for her husband was on the ground floor of the little house they inhabited at the extremity of the village. It was lighted by a large window, opening upon the street. Thick red stuff curtains prevented the curious eyes of the passer-by from looking into the house. A large chest of cherry-wood, a kneading-trough, a cupboard, and a large oak table, composed the furniture. To the left of the chimney, in an alcove, was the bed, furnished with curtains similar to those in the window.

By the unsteady and yellow light of a lamp placed on the table, Jane was knitting. Although she was only thirty-five, the wrinkles on her forehead, and the extreme thinness of her face, gave her the appearance of at least forty-five. Years count double when the heart suffers. Now Jane had suffered much for a long time. She loved her husband, but, alas! Ambrose no longer cared for her. In spite of his ill behaviour, in spite of his cruelty, which increased from day to day, she could not forget that he was the father of her child. Ah! what would she not have given to bring him back to his duty, to make him happy and calm, as in the first years of their married life! But she knew her inability to do so. She wept and prayed, while waiting for the moment when, ashamed of his conduct, Ambrose would repent of his excesses.

Without ceasing her work, Jane listened to every sound without; but she only heard the deep howl of the watch-dog, or the whistling of the wind as it blew wildly against the gable-end of the chimney. Rain and snow—or what we call sleet—was falling; it drove against the door and windows by the violent gusts of wind.

A bitter tear, which had rested on Jane's

eyelid, trickled upon her cheek, and fell on her hand. She raised her eyes and fixed her sad looks on her child, who was kneeling in prayer at a short distance from her. She gazed on her, with a mother's joy, and said :—

" Rose, it is late ; you must go to bed ; you want rest."

The child rose, took a foot-stool, and placing it by her mother, sat down again.

" I assure you, mother, that I am not at all sleepy," said she ; " besides, it is not so late as you think, and I am so happy when I watch with you."

" I do not doubt it, my child; but at your age sleep is so very necessary."

" Well then, mother, let me remain but a little time. You will be so tired of waiting alone."

" Child, I am never alone; do not my thoughts go with you ? Absent or present I see you as you are at this moment—your arms on my knees, your eyes turned towards mine, with your bright smile."

" Then let me remain to watch with you and to comfort you."

" Would you like to remain ?"

" Yes, if you will not be vexed with me."

" Oh ! never, my child."

And the happy mother, forgetting for an instant all her sufferings, pressed her child to her heart. At this moment the clock of the village church struck the hour. Jane listened ; it was eleven o'clock. Her thoughts went back to the absent one. Jane could not conceal her anxiety ; her eyes filled with tears.

" It is eleven o'clock," she said, " and he is not returned."

" The bad weather will have kept him," said the child in a timid voice.

" Yes, yes, you are right, Rose ; had it not been for the rain he had been here long ago."

" You see, mother, dear, you need not cry so."

Jane did not answer, but, wiping her eyes, she said to herself, " God has not abandoned me, for He has given me this angel to console me."

Some minutes passed in silence. Jane, her eyes fixed on the door, trembled at each noise; she desired, even while she dreaded, the return of her husband. She knew but too well what a sad condition he would be in, and she wished to hide from the child the faults of the father; she therefore told her to go to her room. Rose got up in obedience to her mother's request when heavy steps were heard approaching the house.

"It is my father," said Rose.

"Yes, yes, child; leave me."

"It is a week since he kissed me," said the little one; "I must ask him to kiss me this evening; and also, I will beg of him to give me the money you want for me."

"He will not listen to you, Rose; he will be angry that you sat up so long. Go, go away, dear child."

Jane had not ceased speaking when the door opened, and the blacksmith entered. He stopped a minute on the threshold, and looked round as if he did not quite know where he was; then he staggered forward. Jane, trembling, and unable to speak, looked at him with pity. As to the child, she hid herself in the darkest corner of the room.

" Oh, you are not in bed here !" said he.

" I waited for you," said Jane.

" I don't wish you to wait for me; I am free to come home when I please. Am I not master here ?"

" I do not reproach you, Ambrose. Do not be angry ; you have no reason for it."

"Enough, enough; I can't bear complaints."

" You wish me to receive you with smiles when my heart is filled with sorrow. Ah, Ambrose, you are very cruel sometimes ; first complaints, then affection."

" Jane the Good is in the elements. She ought to have another name to-day. I should like to know what."

" Jane the *Miserable*," said the poor woman ; and unable to repress her feelings any longer, she covered her face with her hands, and burst into tears. Rose ran to her mother, and threw herself into her arms.

"Ah, ah, the little one is there, is she?" said the blacksmith. "Rose, come here," added he.

The child approached her father with her eyes cast down.

"Why are you not in bed?"

"Because I wished to see you this evening, father."

"Ah, you wish to see me! I am sure your mother kept you with her."

"No, father; you are mistaken."

"I am sure of it; and I know why."

And he cast a furious glance at his wife.

"And even if it were so," said she, "cannot I have my child sometimes with me?"

"To teach her not to love me," said Ambrose; "to tell her your fancies. Now, Rose, answer me. What has your mother said about me? That I am a cruel father?"

"Oh, father! why do you say that?" said the child in a broken voice.

" Ambrose, how dare you speak thus to your child ?"

" I shall say what I choose to her."

" It is well, Ambrose; since my words displease you, I will be silent. Come, Rose," added she, taking the child by the hand to lead her away.

The blacksmith arose, and seizing the little girl's arm, drew her violently towards him.

" I wish her to remain," said he, and he fell heavily into a chair.

Rose looked at her mother, as if to ask her consent. Jane remained motionless, from fear, but ready to defend her child, if necessary.

" What have you to say to me, child ?"

" Dear father, you know that I am to make my First Communion in a week ?"

" Yes, well ?"

" I must have a white dress."

" A white dress, indeed !"

" Yes, and a veil and a wreath."

" And then ?"

" Mother wants some money to buy all that."

" Oh !"

" You will give her some, will you not ?"

" Some money ? I have none."

" A white dress would not cost much."

" Never mind, you must do without it."

" It is impossible, father."

" You have your Sunday dress."

" But it is blue, not white."

" It is quite new."

" Yes, but it is not *white.*"

" That is no difference to me, you will not have another; I will have no useless expense here."

" Then I cannot make my First Communion," said Rose, sobbing.

" Well, you won't, then; it is all the same to me. Now go to bed."

Rose went away crying. When she was in her room she fell on her knees and prayed fervently. The poor child understood now all the suffering and anxiety of her mother. She knew now why she had so often seen her in tears. Her guardian angel, doubtless, carried her prayer straight to the eternal Father.

In the meantime the blacksmith had fallen into a semi-unconscious state. Jane approached him, and without addressing a word to him, she took off his coat, and helped him to his bed. He was no sooner placed in it than he fell asleep. Jane then took her husband's waistcoat, and from one of the pockets she abstracted a little purse, which she opened. A flush of pleasure passed over her face.

" Rose will have her dress; he has not spent it all," said she.

The blacksmith's purse contained twenty-five francs, half the wages he had received during the last fortnight.

CHAPTER II.

HE day of the First Communion arrived. The evening before Rose Durier had awaited the return of her father, he did not come back till midnight, and Jane, foreseeing the fatigue of the next day, had gently entreated her little girl to go to bed. Rose begged her mother to awake her before her father had left the house in the morning. She wished to ask him something which she hoped he would not refuse her. Jane rose with the sun; she put the house in order, and under her skilful hands the poor furniture looked bright and comfortable. She then went to her child's room, opened a closet, and spread out upon a table the white dress, the muslin veil, and the crown, all of which her little daughter was to wear that happy morning at church.

With what joy she touched these things! Her daughter, her dear Rose, would be beautiful under her clear veil and her white crown, beautiful, above all, in her innocence. With a mother's pride she opened her heart to these sweet joys, and she felt for the moment as if she had never known sorrow.

She approached the bed of her treasured child, opened the white curtains and gazed in an ecstasy of love upon the sleeping angel. In her sleep Rose murmured some words; the mother bent over her to listen.

"Mother, I love you," said the child. Jane pressed her lips upon the white forehead; Rose opened her eyes and extended her arms to her mother as she had done when she was a baby in her cradle. Jane took her in her arms as if she were still a very little child, and began to dress her. A few minutes after the blacksmith entered. Rose ran to him and kissed him, but no sign of pleasure illumined the face of Ambrose.

"Dear father," said Rose, "I have something to ask you."

"What is it about?" said he.

"For some time, dear father, you have not been to church, promise me to go to Mass to-day."

"I have not time, I have something else to do."

"You do not work on Sunday, father; and then I am to make my First Communion to-day, and I should be so happy if I saw you at church by the side of my mother. Say you will come, tell me you will."

"No, I will not."

"Ah! you do not love me, father, since you will not do what I have asked you." And Rose began to cry.

"Rose, my little Rose," cried Ambrose, taking the child in his arms, "do not cry, you know I love you."

Rose smiled through her tears.

" You will come, will you not ?"

" I will see what I can do; I will try."

"Thank you, father; I knew you would do what I asked you."

Ambrose went away, promising his little girl to come back at nine o'clock to put on his best coat to accompany her to church. At half-past nine he had not come; Rose and her mother had been ready for a long while: they were obliged to set out alone.

" He promised me he would come, and he will come," said the little girl.

"He has forgotten it at the cabaret," thought the mother.

Upon this solemn day the modest village church of Cercelle was not large enough to accommodate the crowds of the faithful who flocked to it. The men's benches were occupied by the boys and girls called to the High Feast. All joined with the priest in invoking the blessing of Heaven upon those young heads reverently bowed before the altar. To the solemn chant the organ answered, and the

silver notes of the children raised a joyful
hymn in honour of the Virgin. Then all held
their peace, and amidst the sacred silence all
heads, young and old, bent low.

Several times had Rose glanced around her,
hoping to see her father, but she saw only the
smiling face of her mother.

Ambrose had fully intended to keep his
promise on leaving his wife and daughter in
the morning, but while wandering about, one
of his friends met him, and they went together
to an inn to drink one little glass. But one
did not suffice, and when it was time to go
home in order to keep his promise, Ambrose
found himself so comfortable with his friend
that he thought he might as well remain where
he was at his ease. Besides, a pack of cards
which his companion produced, soon silenced
any little remaining scruple.

Once again before leaving her place to
approach the Holy Table, Rose turned her
head and looked at her mother; the place at
her side was still vacant. Jane was not smiling

now, she wept. After having received Holy Communion, Rose quitted the rails with her young friends, but instead of returning to her place, she left the group, and with downcast eyes and folded hands, she went to the altar of the Virgin. This action surprised every one, all eyes were turned towards the young girl. They saw her kneel down upon the first step and pray with great devotion, her face turned towards the holy figure. In a few minutes she arose and went towards her place among her companions. No one imagined that so simple an action as that of a young girl praying before the altar of the Mother of God could have so serious an effect upon the future life of Rose Durier.

Evening came, but the blacksmith had not come home. However, Jane waited for him; she was sure he would not fail to return, for in honour of Rose's First Communion, he had invited his father and mother (two old people of seventy) to supper with him. Rose helped

2—2

her mother to prepare the two or three dishes destined for the family meal.

" Rose," said Jane suddenly, " you have not told me why you went to pray to the Holy Virgin."

" I thought of you, dear mother, and of my father, and I went to pray for you both."

" Dear child, what did you ask of the Holy Mother ?"

Rose approached her and said, in a low voice :—

" I asked her to make you happier, and to render father worthy of you."

" What do you mean, child ?"

The little girl stammered and blushed.

" Do not scold me, mother, but I know why you cry so often."

" You understand," said Jane. " Alas ! I would fain have kept it from you."

" Take comfort, mother, dear ; in a short time father will be cured of his great fault, he will drink no more."

" God grant that it may be so, Rose."

" Have you confidence in the Blessed Virgin, my mother ?"

" Oh yes, yes !"

" HOPE AND WAIT."

" Yes, we will hope and wait," cried Jane. She opened her arms to the child. " When He sent you on earth, my child, God put into you the soul and heart of the purest angel."

A burst of stupid laughter was the answer to these words. The mother and daughter turned quickly round, the blacksmith was at some paces from them.

" Very pretty," said he, in a mocking tone. " Won't you embrace me ?'

" Oh, in what a state he has come back !" said the poor wife, sighing. " Rose, give your father a chair."

The girl hastened to obey. Ambrose pushed it away with his foot, and leaned against the flour-bin.

" How pretty she is, the little Rose," said he. " You look like a rich young lady. Doesn't she, Jane ?"

"Why, yes," said the mother, pleased at the compliment addressed to her daughter. "This morning at Mass every one admired her."

"And you were not there to see me, father ?"

"True, but it was not my fault—my friends—"

"Ambrose, do not call the men you associate with your friends—say rather your tempters."

"And why so, Jane *the Scold*?"

"Because it is their society that has ruined you. With them you have learned to scorn the most sacred things; your heart has hardened, and you trample under foot the holy faith of your childhood. Are those your friends who keep you away from your home, where your wife, anxious for your future, and that of her child, awaits you in tears ? No; I say it again, those men are not your friends."

"Have you finished ?"

"Yes, for my words are useless. My voice has lost the power of convincing you."

"Well, don't speak to me again; perhaps that will succeed better."

" Oh ! Ambrose ! we might be so happy."

" That's right; now I have a mind to go back again."

" To your *dear* friends, they are so precious ?"

" Yes, for with them I amuse myself—whilst here—"

" You are tired."

Ambrose shrugged his shoulders, and turned away his head.

" Ah ! what's that ?" said he, taking up the wreath that Jane had placed upon the table an instant ago.

" That is my crown, father," said Rose.

" Well, I think your crown, as you call it, is very ugly."

And, looking savagely at his wife, he began to turn it about in his dirty fingers.

Jane took it from him in disgust.

" You are not worthy to touch it," said she.

He seized it, and flung it into the fire. In a moment it was consumed.

" Ambrose," cried the poor mother, " you are a bad man."

Rose wept bitterly.

"Hold your tongue, Jane," cried he, with a menacing gesture. His face wore an expression terrible to behold.

But Jane, exasperated, and driven to bay, as it were, by the brutal action, drew herself up, and exclaimed, "No! I will no longer be silent. Too long have I suffered in secret, and concealed my tears. At last my overburdened heart will speak. The *wife* could be resigned, for her happiness alone was concerned; but to-day I feel that I am a mother, and, as my child suffers, I rise to protect and defend her. The weakness I have hitherto shown has been a guilty weakness. I feel it has in some respects authorized your conduct. If, from the commencement, instead of suffering in silence, I had resisted you—if I had been severe and firm, I should have spared myself much torment, and you a great deal of remorse. Now, the *wife*, though scorned and insulted, forgets all, and forgives you; but the *mother* rebels, and bids you respect your daughter—respect my child."

"Jane, take care, take care," growled the smith, and he raised his arm over his wife's head.

"Kill me if you will; I would rather die than live with such a wretch as you are."

Ambrose growled like a savage beast, and seized a mallet that chanced to be near him. With one bound, Rose sprang between her father and mother, and the blow destined for Jane struck the child on the chest. She gave one cry, and fell senseless into her mother's arms. Some drops of blood oozed from her lips.

"The monster!" screamed the agonized mother, "he has killed his child!"

On seeing the child stagger, Ambrose remained motionless as a statue, his eyes fixed, his mouth open as if a thunderbolt had struck him. Then, suddenly sobered, he fell on his knees—the horror of the crime overcame him. He felt the voice of nature speaking within him; the father knew what he had done, his heart was nearly bursting with suppressed emotion. He sobbed and groaned with anguish as he knelt by the side of his child.

"Assassin!" cried Jane, in a terrible voice— "go away."

Ambrose bent his head. He took in his large rough hands the little burning fingers of his child, and kissed them with deep reverence.

In a few moments Rose opened her eyes.

Ambrose gave a cry of joy. "Saved! she is saved!"

Rose looked at her father for a moment, and then smiled.

"Jane," said Ambrose, "forgive me. From this day forth I swear you shall never have occasion to complain of your husband. I will never drink again."

Rose looked at her mother. She seemed to say, "You see I was not mistaken."

When the old people arrived, the smith was sitting by his wife, with his child on his knee; Ambrose and Jane received them joyfully.

CHAPTER III.

MBROSE did not forget the solemn promise he had made to his wife, in that moment of despair. Not only did he cease his visits to the inn, but he gradually withdrew from the society of his former friends, and at last became as a stranger to them. As he no longer neglected his work he gained more money, and Jane saw with joy that the purse in which she kept the savings began to fill. Grief had aged the poor woman; her new-found joy restored her some years, and with her health her beauty returned. The blacksmith's house, formerly so sad, so silent, was now gay from the early morning when Jane and her daughter sat together in the pretty bow window, now filled with flowers and creeping plants. Often, however, the young girl appeared thoughtful, even sad; her mind seemed to be occupied with other thoughts—it seemed to fly with her soul from the earth. With her eyes fixed on space, her head thrown back, she seemed to hold communion with invisible beings.

It was not long after the day of her First Communion that her mother discovered her in one of these deep meditations.

"What are you thinking of, my child?" she asked.

"Of God, and the holy angels," answered Rose.

And the mother understood that she must respect the thoughts of her child. Sometimes, however, when looking at the young girl, she felt uneasy, without knowing why; her heart had strange misgivings. She said to herself that Rose was very pale, and that her large eyes shone with too great brilliancy. But as the child was growing fast, she tried to attribute her paleness to the effect of the rapid growth.

Four years passed; Rose was seventeen. These four years had been to her four happy fairies; one after the other, as it passed, had left her some precious souvenir. Rose had become as beautiful and graceful as the flower whose name she bore.

After a short illness the blacksmith's father died. Old and worn-out, they expected his death; nevertheless it was a great grief to Ambrose. His mother was very aged also, and overwhelmed by the infirmities natural to her great age, and now she was alone in her cottage. Jane, it is true, passed an hour with her every day; but the rest of the time, could they leave the poor, sick creature alone? Rose asked the permission of her parents to go and live with her grandmother. The smith hesitated, and Jane feared the fatigue would be too much for her daughter's strength; but Rose reasoned them into letting her go.

The poor old woman cried for joy when

she learned that Rose was to come and live with her.

"Was it Ambrose who had this good idea?" asked she.

"No, mother," said he, "it was the child herself who thought of it."

"Come here, Rose," said the aged woman; "know that the only wish I could have, you this day have fulfilled. But I shall not abuse your devotion; I do not wish your bright youth to be passed by the bedside of a sick old woman—to set you free I will pray to die quickly."

"Oh, mother! how can you say that?"

"Do you hear, Ambrose, she scolds me already?"

"She is right, mother. Why speak of death?"

"God does with us as He wills, my son. When He calls me I shall be ready to go to Him. Now, Rose, you are mistress here. My poor little house, and everything in it, is yours. I have there in the cupboard, too, fine pieces of linen of Alsace; you can begin to make your trousseau."

"My trousseau!" said Rose, in surprise.

"That's a good idea, mother," said the smith; "she is seventeen. In a year or two we must think of marrying her. Must we not, Rose?"

She appeared not to hear, but she said in a few moments, "I shall stay with grandmother until she dies, and then I shall belong to the husband of my choice."

The task Rose had undertaken was neither rude nor difficult, but it demanded great care and patience, for Mère Durier was hard to please; she liked to have the girl with her.

"When I see you only, if I only hear you, I forget my pain," said she.

Rose read to her every day for hours. The good priest of the village had placed his little library at her disposal. When the weather was fine, Rose and her grandmother sat in the garden. Their garden was rather large, and produced quantities of vegetables. Two paths divided it equally; they were bordered with strawberry plants. Four large plum-trees, with their thick leaves, prevented the sun from shining too fiercely on the flower-beds. At the end of one of the paths they had made a sort of mound, on which was placed a granite statue of the Madonna.

This enclosure was near a hedge formed of raspberry canes and currant bushes, which grew together, and entwined each other fraternally. It was here that Rose liked to conduct her grandmother, who often fell asleep while listening to the linnets; and Rose, looking at the statue of the Mother of Mercy, sat by her, watching her as carefully as a young mother watches her firstborn. Rose liked flowers; she cultivated the ground around the Madonna, and the plants grew as if by magic. Many people gave the young girl seeds and roots of different kinds. But Rose had gathered her richest harvest from the garden of a rich farmer of Cercelle, a neighbour of her grandmother's. The farmer had a son, aged twenty-two. Whilst he poured into Rose's apron the roots and seeds, he had not failed to remark the innocence and goodness which were visible on the young girl's face, and he knew from the remarks of the villagers that her heart was pure and true. Was she not quoted in the village as the wisest, best, and most pious girl of Cercelle? The young man thought a great deal about it. The old farmer soon perceived that his son was more frequently in the garden, where he had nothing to do, than in the fields, where work never failed. The young peasant, in fact, loved to admire the flowers that Rose tended; he spent long hours standing by the hedge which divided the two gardens. Sometimes he ventured to say a respectful good-morning to the object of his thoughts, and happy indeed was he if she answered him with but a smile! One day he ventured, at the risk of tearing his clothes, to make his way through the hedge, and to enter the widow's garden. He brought a beautiful lily, which he had just uprooted.

"This flower is wanted near the Madonna," said he. This reason was considered sufficient to justify his temerity. Rose was not angry. The lily became the special object of her care, and was soon the grandest flower of the little parterre.

The young man was permitted to come now and then, and chat with Rose and her grandmother. He profited so well by the permission that the opening he had made in the hedge became larger. One morning the farmer perceived it, and easily guessed how it was. He understood now why his son was suddenly so fond of gardening.

"Ah! ah! my son!" said he, "I know your grand passion for flowers, but it is neither wall-flowers, nor tulips, nor camellias that you like the best. It is the Rose, one rose, the blacksmith's Rose. She is young yet; but she is honest and good, and her devotion to her grandmother is admirable. That's something. Come, my son, you have good taste; I am glad to see you are no simpleton."

And the farmer, with his hands behind his back, took a turn round the garden, laughing to himself. The same day he found himself alone with his son in a meadow, where they were cutting the grass. He made him sit beside him on the sweet hay, and then said to him,

"Tell me, Charles, if you know who has made an opening in the hedge between my garden and that of Widow Durier?"

The young man blushed to his ears.

"You do not answer me," said the father.

"I don't think the damage is very great," replied Charles; "but, as you wish to know, I am the guilty one."

"I do not doubt it, my son, for I have seen some very pretty flowers in the widow's garden. I have also seen a charming young girl there."

The young man looked confused, and blushed even a deeper red to the tips of his ears.

"Have you remarked the daughter of Jane *the Wise?*"

"Yes, my father, and if you have no objection—well, Rose shall be my wife."

"I consent in advance. I hope the blacksmith will not refuse us his daughter. I do not think he will find a better husband for her at Cercelle."

"Father, you have made me very happy."

"Rose is not a girl to be overlooked," continued the farmer, without paying attention to his son's words; "her father is a good workman, who earns high wages, and who will save a fortune. And then I know old Mother Durier has four or five thousand crowns well placed out. That will be Rose's one day; the girl is almost rich, and she is certainly the best in Cercelle. Did you know this, my boy?"

"No, father, and to secure her husband's happiness, it is not necessary that Rose should have a fortune."

"To make her husband happy it may not be necessary, but to have a husband at all is another thing."

The young man felt it was best not to

answer; besides, as his father approved of his affection for Rose, he little cared to inquire into his motives for doing so.

"I will see the blacksmith one of these days," said he; "I will say two words to him, and the affair will be arranged."

Charles thanked his father, and they separated—the father to think of his hay, his excellent harvest, and the money he should make this year; the son to dream of Rose, his marriage, and his happy future.

The next day, in the hope of seeing Rose, Charles did not leave the garden, but there was no *rose* among the flowers. He learned in the evening that Mère Durier was very ill, and that her death was expected every minute. She died a few days after.

"Poor Rose," thought Charles, "she must be very unhappy to-day."

And very unhappy he was himself as he stood by the statue of the Virgin and looked at the beautiful lily and the other flowers that the young girl loved so well. The drooping petals fell from the dry stalks—each breath of wind carried off some faded leaves.

"They have not been watered for some days," thought Charles, "another day and they would have withered entirely. Poor little flowers, she loves you so, you shall not die, she shall find you beautiful and smiling when she comes to look at you." So he took a watering-pot, and carefully watered the fading flowers.

CHAPTER IV.

ONE morning the farmer said to his son, "I passed yesterday by the blacksmith's; I thought of you, and I went in."

"Then you have spoken to him!" exclaimed Charles.

"Of course; I had no other reason for visiting him."

"What did he say to you, father?"

"That he was very pleased with the demand, and that he would question his daughter; only he insists that the marriage be delayed a year."

"A year! so long as that?" sighed Charles.

"'My mother is just dead,' said the blacksmith; 'it would not be right to think of pleasure and to rejoice over her tomb hardly as yet closed.' I understood him, and I think he is right."

" It is but reasonable, father; I will wait."

Since the death of her grandmother, Rose had been more dreamy. To see her so languid, one would have thought that she was suffering from great weakness, and that her condition inspired alarm.

Jane often said to herself, "Something is the matter with Rose—a secret thought absorbs her. Why does she not confide in me ?"

" Rose," said the smith gaily, one day, " it appears to me that you have a sweetheart."

"Father, what do you mean ?" said she, quite astonished.

" Yes, yes, and a very well-to-do young man. I heard of it the other day."

" And you tell it me to-day, father, for I did not know it."

" Ah ! you did not know it."

" I cannot understand you, father."

" Are you quite sure ?"

" I cannot be more certain."

"I think you have forgotten; consider a moment."

"I assure you, father, I know nothing of it."

"And yet they tell me that he often talks to you."

Rose turned towards her mother and looked inquiringly at her.

"It was his father who told us," said Jane.

"Charles Bloudel!" exclaimed Rose, and she became paler than usual.

"Ah! ah! you see, you know very well," said Ambrose.

Tears flowed from the young girl's eyes.

"Rose, my child," said Jane, half frightened.

"It is nothing, mother." She wiped her eyes, and then said to her father, "You have seen Monsieur Bloudel. What did he say to you ?"

"That his son wished you to be his wife—he asked you in marriage for his son."

"And what did you answer?"

"That we would talk of it to you."

"Well, father, see M. Bloudel to-morrow, and tell him that I do not wish to marry."

"That you do not wish to marry!" repeated Ambrose, who thought he had not rightly understood the words.

"Yes, father."

"It is impossible," said the smith. "Rose, you must reflect."

"I have already reflected."

"Charles would suit you—I am sure, my child, he would make you happy."

"I think so too, father; he is a good young man, whom I esteem."

"And you show your esteem by refusing him, without pity, without thinking of the pain you cause him?"

"It must be so, father; I cannot be his wife."

"But why? At least tell your father why."

Rose did not answer. A look from his wife gave Ambrose to understand that he ought not to insist, and that there was nothing more to be said then. A few moments after he went out to conceal his annoyance. Jane finding herself alone with her daughter, drew her towards her and said—

" You have vexed your father, Rose ; he is gone out quite cross."

" I am very sorry, dear mother, but I could not answer him otherwise."

" But you could have given him a reason, my child. Perhaps you could not say *all* to your father, but now to me—to your *mother* you can surely confide the cause of your refusal."

" Yes, mother."

" You will tell me why you do not wish for Charles as a husband. Does he displease you ?"

" No."

" Why then ?"

" *Because I wish to be a Sister of Charity, mother.*"

"A sister—a nun ?" cried the mother, with her eyes fixed in astonishment on her daughter.

"Yes, dear mother, in three months I shall enter a convent."

"Is it true you will leave us ? Rose! Rose! you do not love us."

"Oh! mother, you know I do !"

"How coldly you speak of entering a convent," cried poor Jane, in great grief. "Do you know that once the doors are closed upon you, you are for ever lost to us ? We have only you in the world. Rose, you are our joy, our hope ; and you would condemn us to perpetual sorrow. But no ; my tears will move you—you cannot resist a mother's prayers. Rose, we could not live without you—not to see you every day, not to hear your voice! No, it is impossible ; you cannot mean it. Give up this project, it breaks my heart. Besides, your father will never permit you to leave him ; and I know you will not disobey him."

" *You* will help me to gain his consent, dear mother."

" Do not think that ; I will not do it."

" It must be, mother."

" But what has put this idea in your head ?"

" God, mother, without doubt. It was a voluntary vow I made."

" A vow," said Jane, in consternation.

" Yes, the day of my First Communion, when I went to pray at the altar of the Virgin," continued the young girl.

" I remember, my child."

" I thought of you, mother; I had seen your tears; I guessed your sorrows; I knew my father did not make you happy. So I promised to consecrate myself to God, if ever my father became worthy of you, if one day his love for you returned. Heaven has granted my prayer. Now, mother, I must keep my promise."

Jane pressed her child to her heart.

" God has called you to Him," said she, "may His holy Will be done."

She wept, but even in her grief there was joy. For her the sacrifice was made.

The blacksmith obstinately opposed the wishes of his child, although she was supported by her mother; for two months he refused his consent, but at last he yielded; and, accompanied by her mother, Rose departed for the city where the Sisters of Providence awaited her.

CHAPTER V.

ROSE was the joy of the house, the sun-beam that lighted it; her absence caused a void that nothing could supply. Jane forgot her songs; she was silent now; she laughed no more. Sad and thoughtful, she asked herself while sitting at work, "What is she doing now? Is she thinking of us? Is she happy?" Then she looked towards the place where Rose was accustomed to sit, and she gazed until tears filled her eyes, and she could no longer distinguish the familiar objects. It often happened that she thought she heard Rose calling her, and she answered as if the child were near her. When she found out her mistake, she sighed deeply.

Often and often she stood by the little empty bed of her loved child, and thought of her when she was a baby—every article that Rose had not taken with her, she preserved with religious care. "They are my jewels," said she to the neighbours who visited her from time to time. And they spoke of Rose for hours together.

A great change had come over the blacksmith; he was melancholy and silent; he walked about Cercelle like a wandering ghost; his friends who had always admired his gaiety, his good humour, no longer recognized him. He worked at his forge in silence, heated his iron and hammered it without a word, like an automaton. Sometimes he would let the lump of iron, while at a white heat, lie and grow cold again without thinking about it. His workmen said of him, "Ambrose does not work as usual, he has no longer the same energy."

"Why should I kill myself with work?" said he. "I have no portion to save for my child; I am rich enough for myself."

These words were said quietly, but with deep bitterness. However, he little knew that *he* was the cause of his daughter's entering the convent. In hiding the truth from him, Jane had saved him a bitter trial.

The winter that followed was a sad one for Jane and Ambrose. During the long evenings, seated at opposite corners of the chimney, he reading, she spinning, they hardly exchanged a word. And yet they loved each other as much, even more, than formerly, perhaps.

When a letter from Rose arrived at Cercelle, it was a fête day for the parents. One after the other read it, and then it was read aloud by Jane, or her husband, then it was carefully put away in a drawer with the others, but re-read after some days, and if in a short time another letter did not arrive, once again it was fondly read.

One day Jane met Charles in a field. It was the month of March, the country was becoming green. The young man was thin, his cheeks had fallen in, his eyes had lost

4

their brightness, one could see that some deep, bitter grief was wasting him away. He was only the shadow of what he had been. The sight of him grieved Jane.

"Good-day, Madame Durier," said the young man, "you are pretty well?"

· " Yes, thank you ; and you ?"

"Oh! as for me," replied he with indifference, "I desire nothing; I accept what happens to me, good or bad without pleasure, or without pain. Have you heard from Rose ?"

" I went to see her a few days ago."

" How is she ?"

"Pretty well: but I think she is altered— she is so thin ; it grieves me to see her so."

" The fine weather is coming, it will do her good."

" *There*, she does not profit by the weather, poor child."

"She does not speak of returning to Cercelle ?"

" Oh dear no !" replied poor Jane.

The young man turned aside to dash away a tear.

" You loved her well," said Jane, in a feeling voice.

" Oh !" sighed he, " I shall never forget her."

Jane took his hand, pressed it affectionately, and they separated.

Until the end of April, the parents of Rose received a letter regularly every fortnight. But on the 20th of May, that which ought to have arrived on the 15th had not come to hand.

" I feel," said Jane, agitated by all kinds of fears, " that my child is ill."

Ambrose tried to comfort her.

In the evening she told her husband that she should go to the city early the next day.

" We shall have a letter to-morrow," said he.

" Never mind, I shall wait till the postman has passed."

Ambrose was not mistaken, there was a

letter, but the strange handwriting justified Jane's fears.

"*Your daughter is dangerously ill. The superior thinks it her duty to inform you.*"

The carriage which Jane had ordered was at the door; accompanied by her husband, she entered it; they set out together. They did not stop till they reached the convent, the door of which was instantly opened to them.

A sister hastened to conduct them to the sick-room. Rose, calm and tranquil as a Christian supported by faith and piety, lay awaiting her call to the bosom of God. Yes, Rose was dying; but when she recognized her father and mother, her eyes lighted up, and a smile played over her pale lips.

Jane and Ambrose had arrived in time to receive a last kiss; half an hour later, after having pointed to the crucifix to show them from whence she drew her strength, and to where they were to look for comfort, she breathed her last in their arms.

It was as if a thunder-bolt had struck the poor mother; she fell senseless on the floor. The smith, tearing his hair, looked round him with a terrible expression. His grief burst forth in a violent fit of rage. He accused the whole community of having caused the death of his child—"Yes," said he, "the mortifications they have imposed on her have shortened her life. She has died for want of care."

"Do not accuse any one of having caused your child's death," said the good old doctor who had carefully attended the young girl during her illness. "The cause of her illness has existed for years; while very young she *received a blow on the chest*. That *accident* was the cause of her death."

On hearing this, Ambrose groaned deeply, and writhed as though some bodily agony had seized him. His eyes met those of Jane, who had just recovered her senses in time to catch the doctor's words. He could not bear the intense grief which their earnest gaze expressed.

" Oh ! I am cursed !" cried he; "I have killed my child ! I have killed my child !"

" Poor man," said a sister, " his grief has made him foolish."

The superior replied—" His daughter was an angel; she will pray for him."

Jane knelt, sobbing, by the side of the corpse.

In the evening she expressed a wish to take the remains of her child to Cercelle, to have them interred near her. The necessary forms being complied with, this last sad satisfaction was granted her. During that night and the following day they could not persuade her to leave the room where the dead lay. During the second night, the coffin, covered with a white pall, adorned with flowers and a pure white crown, was placed in a hearse. Jane, accompanied by two sisters, set forth, on foot, to follow the body of her child. About a mile from the village, a man suddenly appeared on the road, and placed himself bare-headed by the side of the poor mother.

It was Ambrose who, since the fatal day, had disappeared. Where he had been, what he had done, he did not know himself.

"Jane, Jane," said he, in a broken voice, " can you ever forgive me ?"

"I have forgiven you, Ambrose," answered she ; "the day that you came to me kind and loving, all my affection returned."

"Oh! thank you, thank you; last night I thought I should have died."

"Die! no, no, you must not die, you must live to console me."

The rising sun was gilding the village spire when they perceived the first houses of Cercelle. The curé, who had been informed of what had happened, met the funeral at the entrance of the village. Nearly all the inhabitants had come on foot, and had arranged themselves in silence on either side of the road. A number of young girls, dressed in white, and carrying flowers, were grouped around their banner. Thus, followed by all who had known her in her infancy, Rose was carried to the humble churchyard of her village. A simple stone cross was placed on her grave ; it bore this inscription—

HERE LIES

THE BODY OF

R O S E   D U R I E R,

DIED MAY 21st, 1848.

AGED 18.

The next day, amidst the faded flowers which were scattered on the grave, around the cross, rose a beautiful, fresh-blown lily. The lovers of the marvellous were ready to declare that a miracle had been wrought at the tomb. But it was not the flower alone which excited the wonder of the villagers—below the three first lines of the epitaph, an unknown hand had, during the night, added these words—

"The Village Lily,"

and every one read—

HERE LIES

THE BODY OF

ROSE DURIER,

𝔗𝔥𝔢 𝔙𝔦𝔩𝔩𝔞𝔤𝔢 𝔏𝔦𝔩𝔶,

DIED MAY 21ST, 1848,

AGED 18.

The weather and time have blackened the inscription, but they have not effaced it, and every year, in the month of May, the lily flowers.

THE END.

www.ingramcontent.com/pod-product-compliance
Lightning Source LLC
Chambersburg PA
CBHW022155020726
47496CB00008B/2726

* 9 7 8 3 7 4 2 8 5 7 6 1 3 *